D0230924

This book belongs to:

Dreamcatcher

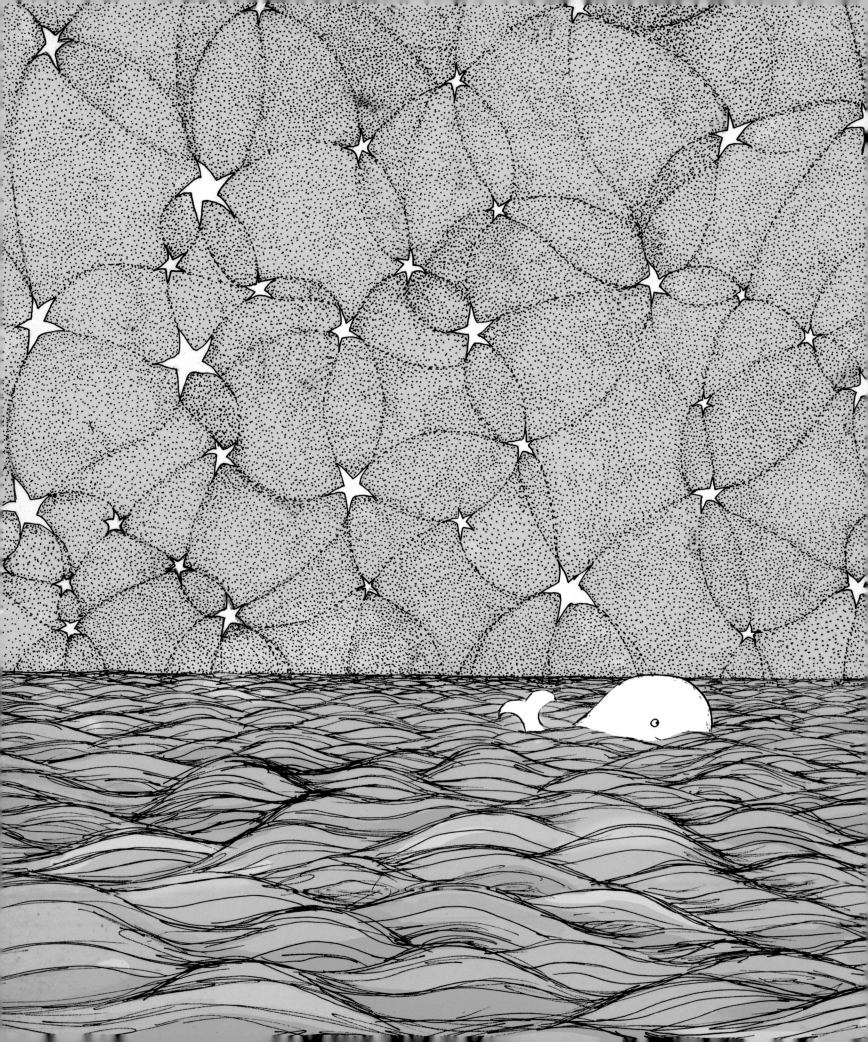

First published in 2012 by Hodder Children's Books.
This paperback edition published in 2013

Text copyright © Geraldine McCaughrean 2012
Illustrations copyright © Maria Nilsson 2012

Hodder Children's Books
338 Euston Road, London NW1 3BH

Hodder Children's Books Australia
Level 17/207 Kent Street, Sydney, NSW 2000

A catalogue record of this book is available from
the British Library.

ISBN: 978 1 444 90466 6
10 9 8 7 6 5 4 3 2 1

Printed in China

Hodder Children's Books is a division of
Hachette Children's Books,
an Hachette UK Company
www.hachette.co.uk

For Jack and Molly with a saucer
of love as big as the moon G.McC.

For Lukas and Elsa with love M.N.

Geraldine McCaughrean

PITTIPAT'S SAUCER OF MOON

Illustrated by Maria Nilsson

Hodder
Children's
Books

A division of Hachette Children's Books

Pittipat was very small,
but he had enormous dreams.
Dreams as big as the moon...

"Under the covers,
no sisters or brothers.
They've gone without me up
to the sky, without a goodbye.
The Moon is a saucer of cream
and they mean to drink it all up.
Well, we'll see about that!"
cried the little cat.

So he climbed into a boat and floated UP, UP,

DOWN

and DOWN,

following drips

and drops of

moonlight

out to Sea.

"You're brave," said the waves, "to reach for the Moon.
That up there, that's a party balloon.
And you with those claws on your kittenish paws.
Reach out to touch it and POP!"

"Not at all," said Pittipat.
"The Moon is a saucer of cream
and I mean to drink it all up."
And tying his tail to a ravel of breeze,
he sailed high and low through
the hillocky seas.

A whale sailed by, spouting aloud, in a silvery spurting, spouting cloud. "Silly kitten! Learn and listen. That old Moon is a macaroon. I like to nibble it, little by little."

Pittipat knew better. "I say the Moon is a saucer of cream and I mean to drink it all up."

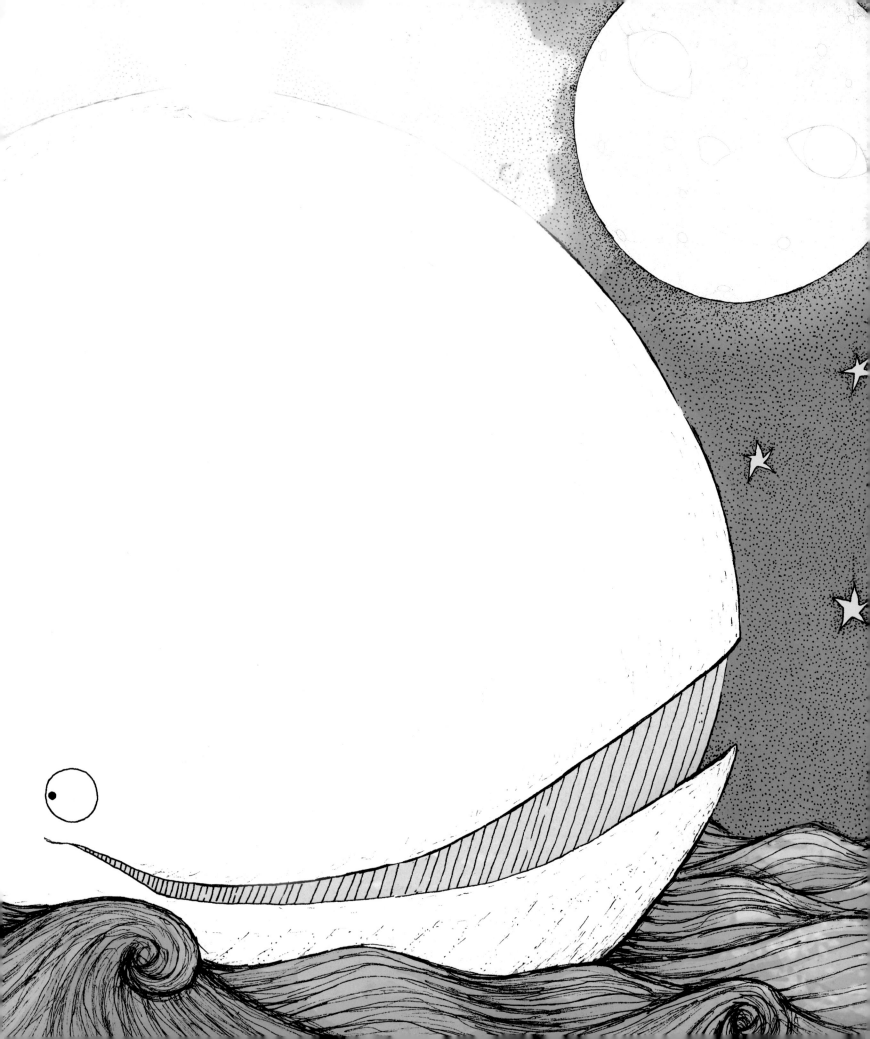

Tucking his tail up out of the wet,
claws sunk deep in the black velvet,
he started to climb the stretchy sky – higher and higher
and higher than high, tearing holes in the gloom
between Sea and Moon.

Soon the Moon itself saw kitten and boat,
"Don't you know, young Pittipat, reckless pussycat?
I am the Naughty Knight of Night who nips cats
and kidnaps kittens. So SCAT Pittipat or join
the others, your sisters and brothers!"
But the Moon had not reckoned with Pittipat,
that wildly daring pussycat. "Huh! The Moon
is a saucer of cream and I mean to drink it all up!"

And the Moon said, "You are rash, Pittipat!
In a flash, little cat, I can bash, crash, clash
and, right or wrong, down you'll
tumble, head over tail, with only
a splash to break your fall!"

"Not at all," said fearless Pittipat.
"The Moon is a saucer of cream and
WE mean to drink it all up."

Now the pale Moon grew even paler with fright –
a milk-white face in a pitch-black Night.
And it blew in their ears to keep them at bay.

"Stay away, kittencats, please stay away!"

"Not us," said the hungry little cats.
"Our brother there, Sir Pittipat,
is the famed moon-drinking pussycat!"
He reached out a paw and drew in his
claws, and a rose-petal tongue ran
round his lips as Pittipat got ready to lick...

But, quick as a flicker, a sliver
of dawn – and a great voice too,
like a grumbling yawn.
"You are purrfectly right!"
purred the big dark Night...

The Moon is a dreamy saucer of cream poured glug glug
from a sky blue jug into a bowl of sky.

Delicious to lick with a quick pink tongue, or stand in,
on all four paddy paws. BUT IT'S MINE NOT YOURS!"

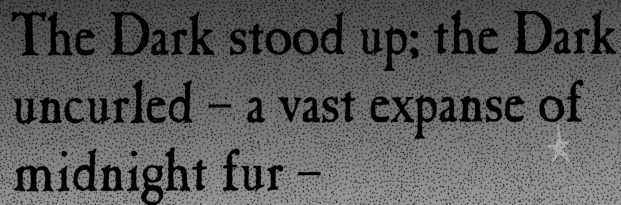

The Dark stood up; the Dark
uncurled – a vast expanse of
midnight fur –

a vaster still expanse of purr grasped each
of her kittens in velvety jaws,

and velvet-pawed

carried each

dreamer...

...back to bed.

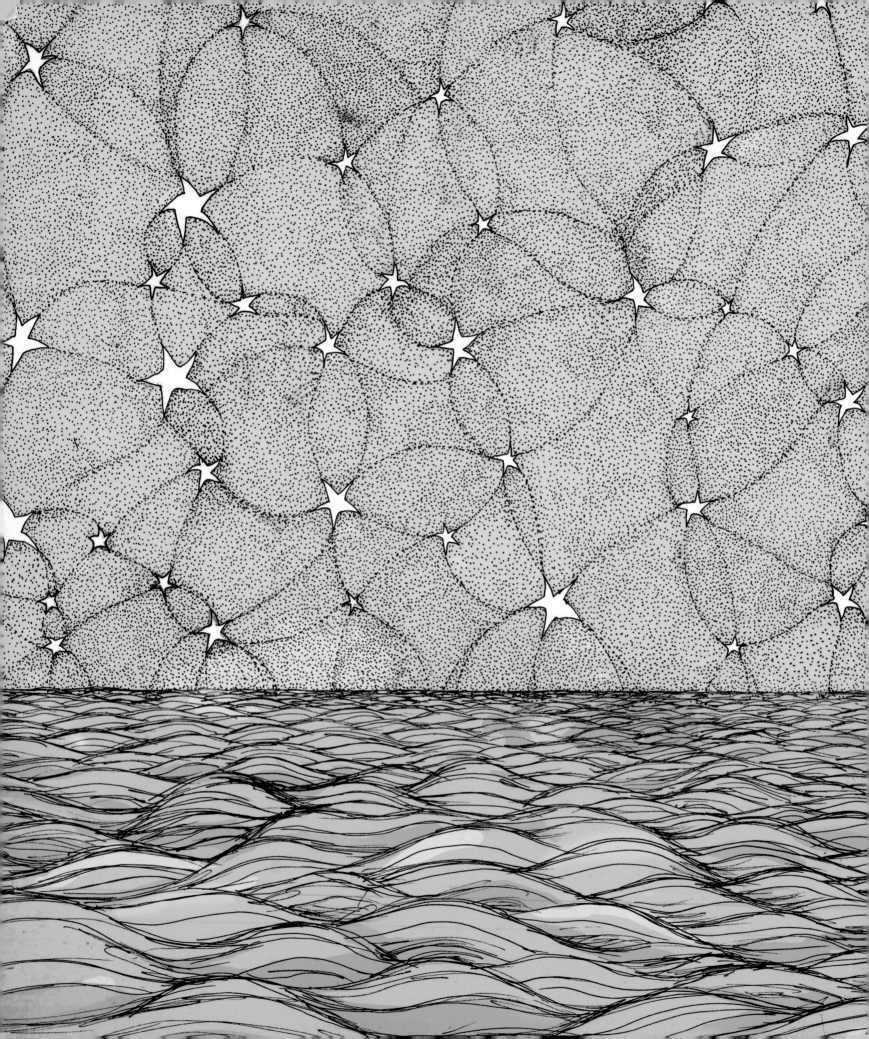

If you enjoyed this beautiful book, you'll love...

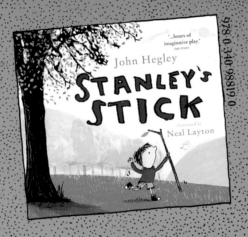